The Tangerine Tree

By Regina Hanson ❧ *Illustrated by* Harvey Stevenson

For
Jackie McLendon
with love, Regina
from JHanson
9.9.95

Clarion Books ❧ *New York*

The author thanks Dr. Fred Gmitter of the University of Florida,
Dr. Julian Sauls of Texas A&M University,
and Mr. Arael Medina of the Flamingo Grove Fruit Company
for providing background information on tangerine trees.

Clarion Books
a Houghton Mifflin Company imprint
215 Park Avenue South, New York, NY 10003
Text copyright © 1995 by Regina Hanson
Illustrations copyright © 1995 by Harvey Stevenson

The illustrations for this book were executed in acrylics.
The text was set in 16/19-point Bodoni.

Printed in Singapore

Library of Congress Cataloging-in-Publication Data
Hanson, Regina.
The tangerine tree / by Regina Hanson ; illustrated by Harvey Stevenson.
p. cm.
5-8.
Summary: When Papa announces that he must leave Jamaica to work in
America, Ida is heartbroken until he tells her a secret.
ISBN 0-395-68963-5
[1. Separation anxiety—Fiction. 2. Fathers and daughters—Fiction. 3.
Emigration and immigration—Fiction. 4. Jamaica—Fiction.] I.
Stevenson, Harvey, ill. II. Title.
PZ7.H1989Tan 1995
[E]—dc20   93-40530
CIP
AC

TWP 10 9 8 7 6 5 4 3 2 1

To Barbara Steiner,
Jane Fitz-Randolph,
and to my parents.
—*R. H.*

For Sophie, with kisses.
—*H. S.*

Ida peeked into the suitcase on the bed. "Why you packin' clothes, Papa?"

"I goin' away for a while," he said.

"Where you goin'?" she asked.

"To New York," said Mama, handing socks to Papa.

Ida patted the suitcase. "Where's New York?"

Her brother Delroy danced her onto the porch. "New York is in America, across de sea. Papa will take de bus to de airplane."

"Can I come with you, Papa?" Ida called.

Papa stuck his head out the door. "Not dis time, sweetheart. Is winter dere now. Is cold and snowy because de sun hidin' from New York."

"So when can I come?"

Papa's forehead wrinkled. "Someday, when we have a little money, maybe we can all visit America together."

"When you comin' back?" she asked.

Basil, her other brother, carried her piggyback to the yard. The hills spun as he wheeled her around.

"Put me down!" Ida cried.

She ran into the cottage. "You comin' back next week?"

Papa shook his head.

"You comin' back for me birthday next month?"

Papa shook his head.

"You comin' back for Christmas?"

Papa wiped his face with his handkerchief.

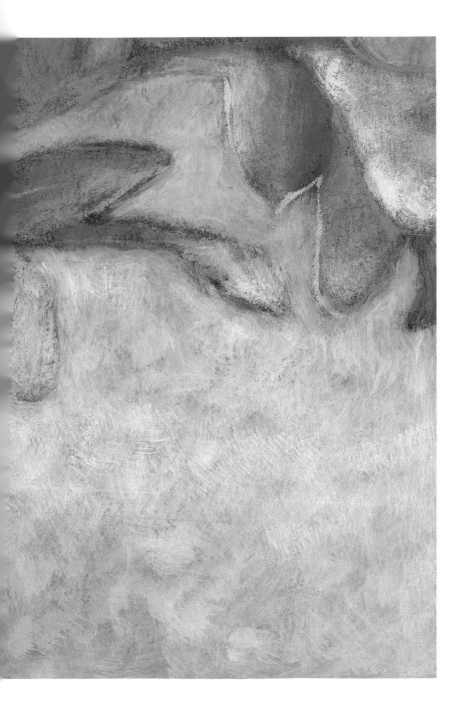

Mama took Ida to sit on the bench beside the hibiscus hedge. "Remember, Ida, what we talk about de other day? Remember Papa sayin' somebody offer him work in America?"

Ida said, "But I didn't think he would stay over dere so long."

"I goin' to miss him, too," said Mama. "You and I will keep each other company."

Delroy propped Papa's guitar on the porch.

"Papa takin' de guitar!" Ida stifled a sob. "He never comin' back!"

Papa came out and put his arms around Ida and Mama. "Of course I comin' back! De whole time I am in America, all I will think about is seein' Delroy and Basil and Mama and me own dear Ida again."

Ida mumbled, "Why you have to go?"

"I can't find work here," said Papa. "In America I'll earn money to pay rent on de house and de land. Money to get school uniforms for you and de boys, and to buy a cow so you can have milk."

Mama said, "We want you children to have a better life dan us, and good education too."

Basil said, "Papa takin' de guitar to play Jamaican music when he lonely in America."

Tears stung Ida's eyes as she thought about losing Papa. She had to run and hide so she wouldn't have to say good-bye. She broke free from Mama's embrace and stumbled toward the low, wide limbs of the tangerine tree.

Ida climbed it and curled into her favorite perch. Today the songs of insects did not comfort her. Nor did the scent of tangerine leaves she had bruised, nor the bright fruit that seemed to set the tree ablaze. She pressed her cheek to the scratchy bark and sobbed.

"Don't cry, Ida." Delroy reached up to stroke her bare feet. "I will look after you."

Basil said, "And I will play with you. We goin' to build a kite—with tissue paper and bamboo."

"I don't want to," she said.

"A hummingbird kite!" said Basil. "With a red beak and two long black streamers for de tail. And you will fly it high, Ida!"

She didn't answer.

Then she heard Papa's voice. "A present for you, Ida girl."

Glancing down, she saw Papa holding up a parcel wrapped in newspaper and tied with ribbon. She said nothing.

He set the present on a nearby limb. "Open it and I will tell you a secret."

Ida hesitated, then unwrapped it. She recognized the old book that once belonged to Delroy, then to Basil. It had a fresh cover of crisp brown paper. She knew its title by heart: *Stories of the Ancient Greeks.*

Papa climbed up beside her. "Dis is our secret: by de time you are big enough to read it by yourself, I will be home."

"But it will take forever, Papa. Dis book too hard for me."

"No-no," he said. "You already know de letters. Mama and de boys will help you with de words."

She clutched the present. A story book of her own!

Papa said, "While I gone, Delroy goin' to care for de banana plants. Basil goin' to see about de yams." He touched the dimple in her chin. "And dere is something you can do for me."

"What, Papa?"

He got down, lifted her onto his shoulder, and walked toward the cottage. "Can you take charge of de tangerine tree, Ida? Can you pick de ripe fruit and help Mama sell dem in de market on Saturdays?"

Ida nodded. "Tangerine trees grow in New York, Papa?"

"I don't think so, Ida. Tangerines grow where de sun shine warm all year. Now, you remember how to help de tree to have de best fruit?"

She nodded again. "I must ask Mistress Sun to sprinkle down little pieces of her fire. De tree will catch de tiny bits of sun and put dem inside de tangerines to give de fruit color and make dem ripe."

While Mama and Ida's brothers helped Papa finish packing, Ida hurried to the cooking shed behind the cottage. She found a bottle and a cork. Once more she ran to the tangerine tree.

Careful to avoid thorns that sometimes grew near the tangerines, Ida picked the ripest fruit from branches that hung close to the ground. "One from Mama, one from Delroy, one from Basil, and dis one is from Ida!"

She peeled the four tangerines and squeezed their juice into the bottle. Some trickled down her arm. Licking it, she tasted the sweet rain and green hills. But mostly she tasted warmth from Mistress Sun.

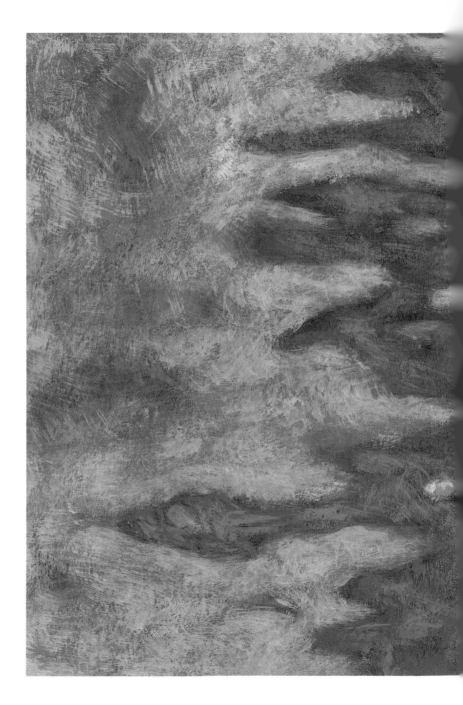

Far off, a bus's horn echoed through the hills. Papa's bus. A lump tightened Ida's throat.

The others came out of the cottage and she joined them. For a few moments Papa gazed all around, at the land that leaped to kiss the sky. She glimpsed a tear on his cheek.

They set off on the path down their hill. Mama went first. Delroy carried Papa's suitcase. Basil carried the guitar.

Papa held Ida's hand. She hid the bottle behind her skirt as they walked past the banana grove, and past the slope where yam vines snaked up poles. By the time they reached the road, Ida heard the bus whining around the corner.

Papa hugged her brothers and Mama. As he clasped Ida to his chest, the bus roared toward them.

"Here, Papa. Take dis with you." Ida gave him the bottle. "I squeeze out sun from de tangerines into it. If New York is cold and snowy when you get dere, dis bottle will warm you up."

With the hem of her dress she dried Papa's cheeks. The bus took him away.

They listened until its echoes faded. Then, silent as the hills, they walked back up their path.

Delroy went to the banana grove, and Basil to the yams.

In the yard Mama stood alone with head bowed.

"Come, Mama." Ida led her to the tangerine tree. The air smelled of the fruit she had squeezed.

Ida got the book from the limb where she had left it. "Teach me to read dis book."

They sat by the tree and sounded out the words. "'Long ago, on an island named Crete, there lived a fearful monster . . .'"

Ida snuggled into Mama's safe lap. "You know what, Mama?"

"What, precious love?"

Ida whispered, "I goin' to know dis book fast. Den I will read all de books Teacher have at school. And den I will write to Papa and tell him it's time to come home."